KINGSTON
A mouse in the
FOREST ZOO

Written by KM Keleher
Illustrated by Tommy Ong
Edited by Tom Kravitz

KINGSTON A mouse in the Forest Zoo
Copyright 2021 GamesPgh, LLC

ISBN 978-0-578-30807-4

For Catherine and Thomas

Sprouts by Kim

Chapter 1

Kingston runs from things other creatures consider as safe. The winter rain slowly soaks the ground. The many, many underground tunnels will without warning, become a rush of water. He watches his friend Shu jumping under a log in the woods. He hopes that log will provide him enough protection.

Kingston crosses the farmer's field to gather birdseed. The sky above will not warn him of the owl's presence. The open field is the owl's cafeteria. Remnants of half-eaten pumpkins lay scattered on the frozen ground. There are some seeds mixed with hoof prints and the scent of a large cat. The wind shifts and Kingston darts for cover.

He waits as the owl swoops and grazes the rock he is hiding behind. When it is safe, he continues to zigzag his way toward the chicken coop. Score! He stuffs as many seeds into his cheeks as possible.

With new-found power in his legs, he makes his way back through the wet tunnel. He pops up from underground and runs back to the tool shed in the Forest Zoo. The tiny opening at the shed door's base is his only way in. Dig! Push!

His body is halfway through. Kingston suddenly feels the ground softly thumping behind him. The vibration and sound get closer as he struggles for shelter. He pushes with his strong back legs, and the door gives just enough.

He's in! Surveying the space quietly, the rain's soft, irregular tapping on the plastic roof is no longer a threat. This is a high, dry place. A discarded piece of insulation in a cardboard box is exactly what he needs for his winter nest. Kingston carefully stores the corn, millet, and thistle in the box corner. He fluffs the insulation into a bed. Kingston closes his eyes for a winter snooze in his new home.

The source of the thumping is unaware of the fear that it caused one little mouse. Mud slushes between her great toes as she sinks inches with every step. Water drips from her massive pile of reddish fur. She prefers to stand on just two feet.

The Forest Zoo wall is sixteen feet tall. The water pours through the culverts to the zoo's storm drain. The drain prevents anything but fish and frogs from going through. The water runoff flows into the stream by the farmer's field. The huge creature picks a low spot where the metal fence meets the tree line. This path leads to the hiker's country store. Stepping easily over this metal fence, a small piece of auburn fur is caught on the wire. A metal object shines in her closed hand as she climbs the hill.

The grinding motor of a grocery truck is the first morning sound of man. It signals dawn as makes its way up the bumpy mountain road. The dim lights bounce off of the early morning rain and fog. The driver squints through the rain spattered windshield. The wipers scrape back and forth removing the moisture from the glass. He remembers last fall, a truck hit a pothole. A crate of peanut butter bounced off into the bushes. The jars were never found. Pressing down on the gas pedal carefully, he rounds the corner.

Abruptly, he applies the brakes. This stops him from hitting what he sees through the windshield. A hairy arm, shoulder, and leg are moving quickly through his headlights. This specter crosses the road, and then disappears into the trees. After the path is clear, he accelerates. He does not want to stick around to see if that thing will come back. The grinding vehicle continues its uphill climb to the camp store. He hopes nothing bounces out of his truck.

Arriving at the store, he greets the owners. He starts a conversation. He asks if a large dog has been loose in the neighborhood. The couple searches each other's faces. They shake their heads no. The driver quickly changes the subject. He finishes his delivery as the rain stops. On his way back down the hill, the dawn sunlight makes everything look less frightening. He turns onto the main road. Breathing a sigh of relief, he sees the village. This last stop will complete his route.

Chapter 2

This neighborhood is across the ocean inlet from a much larger town. People get to work by ferry or commuter bus. Gwen's Mother is teaching. Her stern voice stirs the children from their end of winter distractions. These school students' eyes are on the window, not on the lesson. Spring tugs at them like a friend wanting to play. Katie is new to town. She has red hair and two ponytails. Her parents build apps. She

* Mammal and reptile. By Tatiana Bolshakova

moved to town in the middle of the school year. Katie is still deciding if she likes this place. Getting used to everything is hard. The chill of the classroom is felt on the part of her legs above her socks. She decides she will wear pants for the rest of the school year.

Katie is glad it is Friday. After the bell rings, the children board the bus. She is happy to see her friend Jiang rush in and take the seat next to her. Katie and Jiang start to press the side of closed fists against the steamed glass. They add toes with fingertips to make the moisture footprints.

The ride seems faster with a friend. The next stop is Jiang's. A young woman waits for him as he gets off at his stop. Katie knows this means his parents must be working late at the hospital. Katie hopes Jiang will go to the restaurant tonight. She was too shy to ask him to go. Sophia and Ben told Katie at school that they plan on being there. Sophia's parents run the restaurant. Ben's Father picks up the bread they make there. He then delivers it to local stores. Katie can see her mother waiting at the stop. The bus door closes behind her. They make their way out of the cold and into their new home. There are boxes in the living room waiting to be unpacked. Katie enters her bedroom. She is surprised to see that her bed is set up.

Bright curtains are hanging and a few boxes remain. She knows that her comfortable pants are inside one of those boxes. "Mom, can we go to Sophia's tonight?" "Sophia?" Her mother asks from the other room. "Yeah, the restaurant, everybody goes there." "When your dad gets back from the store, we will ask him." Katie continues the search for her pants. Fifteen minutes later, Katie is fully dressed. She stands in her hat, coat, boots and pants waiting by the door.

This greeting surprises her father. He enters the house holding a bag from the electronics store. After a brief discussion, Katie and her parents drive to the restaurant.

Katie and her family are seated in a booth right next to Lucas and his dad. Lucas has thick brown hair. Katie doesn't know him very well. He sits two rows behind her at school. He always plays basketball on the playground with Ben, Jiang and Gwen. Lucas notices Katie right away. He gives her a half-smile and a nod. Katie returns the gesture. Katie gets out of her seat to read the Wi-Fi password from the dry-erase board next to the cashier. She sees Sophia is folding napkins. Katie realizes this restaurant is named after her. Ben is seated in the back room with his family. On the way back to her seat Lucas says "Katie, text me!" They quickly exchange numbers.

When sitting back down at the table Katie receives a text from Lucas on her phone. "Katie, we are here to eat," Her father reminds her. When the waiter arrives she announces; "I'll have the spaghetti, please." "From the kid's menu," Her mother adds. While she waits, she sees Lucas popping fries into his mouth. On the back of his forearm is a large bruise. While her parents talk, she texts under the table. *Hey, where did you get that bruise?* Katie puts her phone on silent mode and waits for his response. *The tree I was in was slippery. I had a crash landing by the zoo wall.* He answers back. Texting while eating is not allowed. The food arrives at the table. Katie slides her phone into her pocket and stirs her spaghetti with a fork.

Katie's weekend is spent getting her room in order and saving her text contacts. This new place seems suddenly full of life.

The next Monday feels completely different for Katie. She is dressed in her warm pants. Having the contact phone numbers of Lucas and his friends now makes her part of the group. Her phone is tucked away in a safe place. The school lessons are much more interesting. Gwen's Mom reviews the differences be-tween mammals and reptiles. Yanu's seat is to Katie's right. She is busily making a wild cartoon of mammals and fighting rep-tiles. Yanu sees Katie watching her draw. She looks up and smiles. Yanu has dark curly hair, dark brown eyes, and tiny spar-kling earrings. In her cartoon, she has made the mammal a huge creature. It has large feet. It is carrying an alligator by its tail with one hand. It is holding what looks like a cell phone in the other hand. Sophia is sitting one row behind both of them. She cannot resist a glance at the interesting artwork. The teacher's voice booms "Sophia, name one reptile!" All three girls jump a lit-tle in their seats. They are all now looking to the front of the room. Sophia with her long dark curls answers "Alligator!" This was too much to hold back. The three of them start to giggle. This makes most of the class laugh. The teacher, wanting to refocus the room, asks Katie; "Name one mammal." She is ready with her answer; "Gorilla!" This quick, correct answer brings more laughter from the class. The bell rings. The teacher speaks over the bell. "Tomorrow there will be a quiz. There will be questions on small reptiles and mammals as well as the large ones."

The bus ride home can be pretty boring, or fun depending on who is there. Jiang and Katie get to work making hand footprints on the bus window. Yanu jumps into the seat behind them. She watches through the gap in their seats. Jiang and Katie look back. "Hey, Yanu!" Katie says. Yanu smiles and asks; "Did you see the footprints too?" Both children think about her question for a minute. Jiang asks; "You mean these?" "No," Yanu says. "Big ones, you can see them in the mud all around our store." This comment brings a look of surprise from both of them.

Katie is now planning a reason to visit the hiker's supply store. Yanu opens a photo on her phone. The three children pass the phone around. Jiang almost forgets his stop. He passes the phone to Katie, and then gets off of the bus. Katie's stop is next. Katie hands the phone back. She steps off to greet her mom. She turns to wave to her classmate. Yanu looks back from the bus window and waves. The bus makes its way up the bumpy mountain road to the last stop. Yanu steps off of the bus. The door closes behind her.

She sees her father on a ladder clearing the winter leaves and sticks from the gutter. He turns to nod at the bus driver. He smiles at Yanu as she runs toward the ladder. "Dad, do you see the footprints?" Through water- splashed glasses he looks. He squints and sees nothing. Yanu is pointing at several places on the ground. The last footprint stops at the store wall, close to where her father has his ladder propped. Her father pulls out a scoop of muddy leaves. He aims and tosses the dirt onto the plastic sheet by the base of the ladder.

There is a clinking sound of metal hitting the rung before dropping to the ground. Two pale gold objects held together by a circle shine through the mud. Yanu quickly reaches for the cause of the sound. "Wait, don't," her father cautions. Carefully he steps down from the ladder. With a gloved hand, he fishes through the muck, and retrieves the object. With thumb and index finger he holds the two pieces of metal up to see. The objects look like heavy earrings to Yanu. "What are those?" Yanu asks. "Keys," her father answers. "The keys are to what kind of car?" Yanu asks again. "No car, he smiles, these keys are to some old building." Yanu persists,

"Now do you see the footprints?" Her father wipes the keys and places them into his pocket. He removes his glasses to wipe them, then, he puts them back on his face. He examines the ground leading up to the ladder.

There are many of his boot prints visible. Some boot prints cross large, weird footprints. The last large footprint stops at the side of the store wall. "Very funny," her father says. "How did you do that?" "Do what? I just got here and I am wearing shoes. They were here this morning too! I took a picture while I waited for the bus." Yanu shows the picture to her dad. He has a look of concern on his face. He looks around, and then tells his daughter to go help in the store.

The next morning, just before sunrise the delivery truck arrives. This time Yanu's parents are the first to speak. They ask Ben's Father if the large dog he saw the other day had strange feet. This conversation leads to the adults looking at the ground outside of the building. Ben's Father explains that the rain and fog made it hard to see. He gives his best description of what he saw in those conditions. The adults reluctantly agree that it wasn't a dog. The rest of the day the strange visitor is first on everyone's mind.

Yanu's parents install cameras all around the building. In the mornings Yanu now waits inside the store and is then walked to the bus. Ben's Father remembers when the zoo was a fun place for everyone. Now he must warn his son not to play by the road, or near the abandoned zoo.

Chapter 3

Springs' invitation to play changes everything. The students notice the sun coming up a little earlier and setting a little later each week. The earth's frost softens. Small green seedlings are visible in places. It is a Saturday in April. The friends send each other a group text; *Meet at the stream by the zoo.* The children tell their parents they will all stay together. The parents give consent. Gwen is a year older. She is known as the responsible one. Jiang's Parents can see the stream from their house. Ben's Father drives the delivery truck. He remembers his father's strict instructions to not play in the zoo. Or was it too close to the zoo? The stream seems far enough away for Ben.

Lucas shouts above the water pouring from the zoo storm drain, "Gwen, look!" He throws a stone; it skims the water's surface 3 times.

The rock stops at the edge of the stream. Lucas is on one side; the rest of the children are on the other.

Katie carefully chooses her rock based on how it fits in her hand. Her stone is smooth with a thin edge. She throws the thin side first toward the water. She makes two big skips in Lucas' direction, then a splash before sinking. Gwen is standing in her skirt, shorts, and sweatshirt. Her blonde hair is pulled back in a ponytail. She folds her arms and watches. She counts points for the number of skips, and starts keeping score. The rocks that skip high seem to get more attention. All of the friends begin skipping rocks.

This makes scorekeeping difficult. Some rocks hit each other midair as they skim across the water's surface. Rock skipping turns into rocks colliding. Lucas removes his jacket. Katie notices the bruise on his arm is fading. Katie asks Lucas "Which tree did you fall out of?" "That one," answers Lucas, pointing to a fir tree on the hill close to the zoo wall.

"Now that it isn't raining, maybe I can try it again. If I climb high enough, I may see over the wall." "My father said I can't play in the zoo," Ben warned. "We won't play in the zoo. We will just get a picture from the tree," Lucas answered. Jiang spoke up. "My parents flew a drone over the zoo. It crashed into a tree inside the wall. Later that day, we found it broken, outside the zoo wall."

The final photo saved on the SD card was teeth, some animal tongue, and a picture of a dog's nose. At this point, the children's eyes are wide. Their faces have a mix of curiosity and fear, more curiosity than fear. Since Katie is new, they give her the zoo's history. The zoo was abandoned by the owner. He hung a CLOSED sign on the gate and left with haste. The location of the zoo keys and owner is a mystery to everyone. Some of the animals may or may not still be there. During the day this is a fun place to play. On windless nights the pumpkin farmers' dogs bark in the direction of the locked, rusted zoo gate. Without many words, the group runs to the fir tree.

This time, Lucas isn't climbing alone. With a group of friends, it is easier. Just like the ninja cartoons Lucas and Gwen liked to watch. Lucas hugs the base of the tree. Gwen takes off her shoes and stands in her socks on Lucas' shoulders. The third tallest is Jiang. Jiang completes the shoulder stand. First Lucas, then Gwen offers cupped hands for him to step into. Jiang is passed up the tree quickly. He is able to grab two smaller branches. Finally, he grabs one big enough to support his weight. To his surprise, he can just see over the zoo wall. Gwen says, "Hey, maybe by testing our skills, we will all discover our superpowers!" The friends think about this as they play lookout for Jiang.

"Can you see?" He knows this is like riding his bike. He cannot lose his balance. Carefully he leans his back against the tree trunk. He straddles the branch with his legs. He turns his head to his friends and answers. "I can see everything." He slides his hand carefully into his pants pocket to retrieve his phone. "I will get a picture."

The view from the tree reveals a weird mix of chaos and beauty. Pale green sprouts cover the paw and hoof furrowed ground. Empty food jars and discarded packaging are strewn across the mud. Pink and white metal boxes form a trail from the broken window in a small building marked "GIFT SHOP." On the far side of the zoo, on the soft earth, scattered among empty peanut butter jars, lies a broken metal door. It is like a dog cage door at the pet store, but much larger.

There are little wooden houses with fading paint. Even during the day, Jiang thinks, this place looks spooky. "Get a good one," the children below cheer! Jiang hugs the tree branch hard with his legs to free his hands and lifts his phone. His nervous finger taps the camera icon. The screen opens up to reveal a good view of everything. He snaps four photos. Abruptly, the phone vibrates in his hands.

Fearful, he sees his mom is calling him. Jiang yells down to his friends. "I got four pictures. My mom is on the phone, shhh." He motions with his finger to his lips. Jiang takes the call from the tree. He explains everything is fine. His mom wants to know why she cannot see him, or his friends at the creek. He explains that they went looking for better rocks to skip. Whether she believes him or not he is un-sure. He hangs up and shouts down to his friends, "We have to get back to the creek so mom can see us." No one wants to get into trouble.

Lucas and Gwen resume the stance. They form a shoulder stand against the tree. Jiang drops down to the smaller branches, then steps into the cupped hands that wait for him. He steps safely onto the ground. At that moment they realize together, they form a special team.

The friends run back to the creek. Jiang remembers what he told his mother. He picks up a slightly flat, smooth rock for skipping. Making his words the truth, he tosses the stone into water. He then sends photos as a group message. They all promise to keep the pictures a secret. They continue playing by the stream until they are all wet and hungry. The friends agree to meet again tomorrow.

Everyone goes to bed that night studying the zoo pictures that Jiang took from the tree. Each one wonders what their superpower might be? They also wonder about the shadowy creature in the zoo photo, watching from behind the branches.

Chapter 4

The Sunday afternoon is bright and warmer. Everyone had arrived home soaking wet the day before. The friends agree to meet the next day in a dry place. They decide on the basketball hoop right behind Sophia's Restaurant. Ben, Jiang, Gwen and Lucas jump right into shooting hoops. The smaller friends sit at the outdoor table looking at the mysterious pictures. These pictures are still a secret from everyone but them. Katie enlarges the photos. A dark round head with an ear becomes visible. Yanu sees a shadow where an eye may be. A dark curled stick appears behind the head. Sophia says, "It's a giant worm." "No wonder the zookeeper ran away," adds Katie, laughing.

The girls consider what may have happened. Katie knows that even an old zoo should have a website. She searches for forestzoo.com, she gets nothing. She tries forestzoo.org. To the girls' surprise, a website with a picture of the zoo when it was new is visible. There is a link to download the app. Katie taps the link. "Wow, it actually works." The app opens to a game. A large set of antique keys are visible. In the background, there is a picture of the locked zoo gate. While the girls are studying this, Yanu recognizes the strange old keys as the ones her father found in the mud.

Lucas reaches into his jacket pocket for his earbuds. He realizes they are missing. He stops shooting hoops as he fumbles through his pocket. Jiang and Gwen ask, "What's up?" "I think I left my buds somewhere," Lucas answers. "You had them yesterday," Gwen reminds him. "Maybe we should go back to look," Sophia adds. "I have my bike here. We can ride down." Remembering the buds were a gift; Lucas accepts Sophia's offer to look for the earbuds to avoid trouble. Sophia gets permission from her parents. Lucas sends his father a text. He agrees to let him go as long as he is back by noon. Sophia gets her bike. She offers her brother's bike as a loaner. The children take turns shooting hoops as they watch Lucas and Sophia ride off.

Approaching the creek, they know they must not ride over the small earbuds. They drop the bikes on the rocky slope and step toward the creek with caution. A few drops of rain fall from the sky. This dampens their caps and jacket sleeves.

In the forest, spring rain sounds like winter rain to Kingston. His dark winter home does not share the light of the longer days. The tapping of rain on his shed roof is interrupted by sudden blinding light everywhere.

Kingston stands with his back against the cardboard box. One eye is closed in the brightness. With the other eye, he sees a huge silhouette. His strong back legs spring into action. OUT he runs, out the door, past the huge dark figure. His friend Shu is several feet away. Shu and his friend peek from their winter nest. Pointed noses and whiskers twitch cautiously from the hollowed log. Their dark, watchful eyes see Kingston. They hope he is making the right move.

The mouse is running for his life. He makes his way straight ahead. The quickest exit is the zoo storm drain. Kingston slips and slides in the mud. He falls, gets his footing, then he slips again. The items nabbed from the gift shop lay scattered by the stream. He grabs for a small branch; it breaks in his paws. He falls downward. He hits something hard, and not familiar to him. It is a small metal box. As he lands, it snaps shut, creating complete darkness. He feels spinning and falling, then the sound of water. As the liquid seeps in, Kingston scrambles to stay dry.

Sophia sees the small white earbuds between some rocks. She calls out to Lucas. "Hey, I found your buds." Lucas is about to step toward her. An object shoot-ing through the water pouring from the storm drain catches his attention. The pink box is small against the white swirling stream. It disappears into the water for a moment. Then it pops back up. Sophia picks up the earbuds and places them into her pocket. She walks toward Lucas who is now focused on this man-made, floating object. It bobs helplessly in the deepest part of the stream. "What is that?" asks Sophia. "Let's get a stick," Lucas answers.

Standing carefully on the stream's edge, they snap off a green tree branch. As they reach for the object, the branch bends. It is hard to control. With each swipe, the box moves slowly away from the center of the stream. But, with each stroke of the branch, the box sinks a little. Sophia and Lucas move the branch faster. It finally gets close enough to them. They hook it in the rest of the way. Lucas bends over and grabs the plastic handle connected to the lunch box with two metal rings. It feels heavy. The water pours out of the crack between the box and the lid. Then the box tilts on its own in his hand. The sound of frantic scratching against metal is heard. Lucas stoops to set the box on the ground. Sophia bends to look. "Be careful Lucas, just peek first."

Lucas opens the box a crack. Instantly, two black eyes and whiskers are visible. A thin metal gold band can be seen tipped over one ear. "Eeep!" Sophia squeaks. Lucas shuts the lid. "Wow! He's like a pet," Lucas says quietly. The sprinkle of rain starts again. "We better get back. My bike has a basket. I can tie the box with my hairband," Sophia says as she rolls her eyes. With a grin, she hands Lucas his earbuds. Lucas remembers to zipper his pocket this time. They take the smoothest trail back. It is 11:50 AM as they return to the basketball court.

Their friends watch them as they ditch the bikes in the bushes. Sophia is holding up a pink metal box. "Did you find the buds?" Ben asks. "Oh, yeah," Lucas answers as he pats his pocket.

Sophia is reluctantly holding the metal box that is jiggling slightly. They drop the basketball and run over to see this weird thing. "Quick, my father will be here any minute!" Lucas says as he reaches out for the lunch box. Sophia quickly passes it to him. "I'll tell you later how this goes." Right on time, Lucas' Father arrives in a dark green car. Lucas covers the box with his jacket, opens the passenger door and gets in.

Lucas leaves Sophia to explain the contents of the metal box to her friends "It is a mouse wearing a gold ring on its head." This makes everyone laugh. Sophia tries to make her friends believe that she is not joking. Holding up her phone, she reminds them to look at the odd things in Jiang's zoo photos. They notice the pictures show items scattered in the zoo's yard. A mouse wearing the gold band on his head still seems too strange to be real.

Chapter 5

Lucas is busy in his room while his father is getting lunch ready. He quickly enters his closet and pulls out an empty fish tank. It once was home for a snapping turtle. His father made him put it back into the creek after just one week. This time, maybe a mouse will make a better pet. While kneeling on the floor, he lays a brown paper bag to cover the glass bottom. He pulls some stuffing from a tear in an old pillow. This will be the bedding. As a finishing touch, he adds a cardboard toilet paper tube. Lucas can hear his father clattering plates in the other room.

He kneels and carefully unwraps the metal box. He pulls up on the latch. He lifts the lid and flips the box upside down over the glass aquarium. He can hear drops of water hitting paper. He hears a small "Thunk!" followed by the sound of feet scrambling. Lucas fumbles for the lid. He quietly slides it over the top. Through the lid holes, he sees two eyes looking up at him and a tiny, nervous, wet body. The small gold band is still stuck over one ear. Lucas' attention is drawn to the smell of food coming from the kitchen. Lucas grabs his phone and takes a picture of the mouse. Even wet, he knows his friends will think this new pet is cool. While his father is standing at the sink, Lucas grabs a few peanuts and crackers from the cabinet. He returns to his room to drop them into Kingston's aquarium. He watches the mouse approach the snacks, stashing a peanut into his cheek. Kingston gets to work quickly fluffing the pillow stuffing into his bedding.

Lucas walks into the kitchen feeling excited. He thinks lunch will be good for both of them. Sliding a chair out, he sits down with his dad. Lucas' Father takes the outdoors seriously. He is a biologist. Lucas isn't sure how he will ask permission to keep this mouse. During lunch, he considers finding food for his friend. The grilled cheese sandwich and soup are good. He knows this is not mouse food. Neither are crackers. From his seat at the table, he spots the bird feeder just outside of the window. He smiles.

That evening, the picture of the mouse with the crown is received first by Gwen. She then forwards it to Jiang, Ben, Katie, Sophia and Yanu. *See, I told you, the mouse wearing a crown is real.* Sophia sends in her text. *He's still a secret until I ask Dad.* Lucas replies.

Knowing his dad may find his friend while he is at school, Lucas chooses bedtime to ask. "Dad, can I get a pet?" "Pets are a lot of work," his father answers. "If the pet is small, it may not be a lot of work, Lucas answers." Remembering the snapping turtle, his father asks, "Okay Lucas, what did you bring home?" Relieved and nervous at the same time Lucas answers, "A pet mouse!" A blank look on his father's face changes to a look of worry. Without saying anything he stands up and walks into Lucas's room. Lucas follows him. His father's eyes sweep the now neat bedroom. "Where is it?" "I'm keeping him warm by the bed," answers Lucas. He then lifts the bedspread up to reveal the aquarium. The mouse had been in the process of stuffing food into his cheeks. Once again, bright light startles him. Lucas and his dad are amused at the appearance of this small creature.

The little mouse is standing on his hind legs. The gold metal band is tilted over one ear. His cheeks bulge on both sides. "His name is Kingston. See his crown?" Lucas explains. "That thing on his head... are you sure a mouse needs a crown?" his father adds. "He had it on when he was in the lunch box," explains Lucas. His father shakes his head with a look of annoyed puzzlement. Lucas pulls out his phone and takes a better picture of his now dry, fluffy, fat-cheeked friend. "Lucas, let's see if he lets us remove his crown."

Lucas' Father washes his hands and digs out a pair of gloves he uses for work. Without hesitating, he reaches into Kingston's aquarium and gently captures him with one hand. He pulls the metal band off of Kingston's head. The mouse's fear and confusion are replaced with apparent relief. To be safe, the mouse hides in his cardboard tube. Lucas adds drinking water and a little more bedding. He then secures the ventilated lid. Lucas asks his dad if his mouse can stay with them.

His dad explains that they will talk about it in the morning. Lucas thinks his father likes his new pet. He goes to sleep listening to his mouse tapping the cardboard against the paper.

The next morning over breakfast, Lucas explains the lunchbox, the mouse, and the stream. Lucas hopes for his father's approval. As they rush to the bus his father says, "We'll talk about it after school."

Lucas' Dad starts his morning video chat. He is talking with his mom. She is working in Alaska. He holds the phone to the aquarium. She can see the small creature performing his favorite activity, stuffing his cheeks. Lucas' Dad holds up the battered, retro lunch box. He explains how Lucas found this mouse in the stream, in this box. "This is another weird discovery from the Forest Zoo," Lucas' Mom says. Both parents notice the mouse's pinkish-white belly. At the base of each ear are patches of lighter colored hair. The ability to store so many seeds in both cheeks is a trait not found in barn mice. Both parents must end the conversation to go to work. They both agree to find out what type of mouse has joined the family.

Chapter 6

The adults have been preparing for some town meeting about the Forest Zoo. The school friends download an app that was linked to the old zoo website. This app plays a video game that shows animals playing catch. The objects being tossed are big, old keys. The animals toss, kick and head-butt the keys. Then a large crea-ture with red fur arrives. It deeply growls "Yeren." The creature takes the keys and walks away with them. When the friends sign on, they are assigned avatars in the game. They play the game over and over. As the players' skill against zoo animals improves, it takes longer for Yeren to show up. Yanu knows the keys in the game look like the ones her father found. The game seems too real for her. Frightened, she plays it anyway, not wanting to give away her secret. The game helps her feel as if she is now part of a team. She is getting better at noticing details that help her win in the game. She finds these skills help her in real life. When she draws things from nature, they now show more detail. As she plays, she notices the animal opponents have different skills. Yanu noticed that even in the game, sometimes the animals left marks on the ground.

Tracker Yanu

This Saturday the friends meet at the stream. They are hanging out with Jiang's Father while most of the adults are at a town meeting. The adults are meeting with some officials that want to enter the Forest Zoo. Lucas' Father told him his new pet would attend the town meeting. Lucas thinks this is funny. His dad must really like his mouse. Maybe the boring meeting will be like an adult show-and-tell.

While playing in the stream, the friends compare their scores from the video game. They share that their game icon under-stands them in some way. Ben is always aware of the rules. His avatar is an adult version of him as a rebellious looking cow-boy. Yanu's game character is a Navajo tracker. Katie's hooded icon is a hacker. Jiang is a robot-dragonfly. Gwen's avatar is a ninja. Lucas is a zookeeper in ankle-high boots. Sophia is a fairy with a tiara. These symbols were assigned by the game when they signed in.

Safari Lucas

Fairy Princess
Sophia

Since these symbols were not chosen by the player, this makes Yanu afraid enough to speak up. She tells Jiang and Katie, "The game says that I am a tracker. I really found the footprints next to our store." Sophia says "I am a fairy princess with a tiara. I found a mouse with a crown." Jiang reminds them, "Our drone was really wrecked at the zoo!" Yanu shares more, "We really found the keys from the game in our rain gutter." Yanu's words stopped all playing by the stream. Lucas, wearing his boots, climbs out of the water. Gwen steps out of her acrobatic side flip. Everyone waits for Yanu to explain the location of the keys. She shows them the pictures from her phone. Yanu feels like she is on the edge of a powerful knowing. The possibility of disappointment is also scary. Katie sees this on Yanu's face and says, "I had been planning on a visit to your store. I would love to see those footprints." "Maybe we can see the keys. The ones you found in the rain gutter," Ben adds, thinking Yanu has been looking a little spooked.

The friends stop playing and decide to go to Yanu's country store. Jiang's Dad watches his son cross the lawn between the house and the stream. Jiang bursts in the door and asks; "Dad, can we get those trail snacks they sell at Yanu's store?" Jiang's father looks out to see the rest of the group sitting on his steps, sending messages on phones. They arrive one by one to Jiang's door and show their parental approval texts. Yanu tells them, "My uncle is minding the store. My parents are at that town meeting. My uncle said he would treat." Jiang's Father doesn't want to seem rude. He has an actual urge to get a snack himself. Jiang's Father agrees.

The car is at the meeting with Jiang's Mom. The friends load into Jiang's beat-up camper. They drive up the bouncy mountain road to the hiker's supply store. He parks and the friends jump out. Jiang's Father and Yanu's Uncle nod and say hello. Yanu's Uncle points to a table that he has set up. The snack bags are waiting. The friends thank him, take the snacks, and sit on the log bench outside. Jiang's Father takes a minute to pick up a few other things. Yanu makes an excuse to look for the keys in the place she knows her father laid them. Yanu tells her uncle "I want to show Katie my room." Her uncle nods. The girls exit the back of the store into a hallway. This leads to the house.

They approach her parent's bedroom. Yanu squeezes Katie's arm. With wide eyes, Yanu whispers, "In here. My father laid the keys on the dresser." Both girls walk in quickly and quietly. The dimly lit room has wooden furniture and wool rugs. Yanu drags a chair to the dresser and steps onto it. Katie enters the room halfway. She is looking over her shoulder, watching the open doorway. Then she looks to the open window next to the dresser with the torn mud-streaked screen. Just at that moment, Yanu groans quietly, moving things around on the dresser top. She then turns around, looking upset. "They're gone, the keys are gone. There's mud everywhere." Katie says, "Yanu, look at the screen." Yanu turns and lets out a muffled shriek. She holds her hands to her cheeks, standing on the chair. "There's mud there too!" Katie adds in a really loud whisper. "We have to go!" Yanu warns. She jumps off of the chair and pushes it back to where it was.

Both girls instinctively head to the hall-way. Their shoes pound the floor as they run. Yanu and Katie burst through the back door, into the store. They surprise Jiang's Father and Yanu's Uncle. Ben and Sophia notice the commotion. They stand up from the log and come inside to listen. Yanu speaks up and says "Uncle, there has been a break-in." Katie's eyes are wide.

She nods her head in agreement. Her uncle asks, "What is missing, what happened?" Yanu answers, "It's the back window, in mom and dad's room. The screen is all torn and muddy," "It's probably just an animal," Yanu's Uncle reassures her. "While we check, wait with your friends outside in the camper." Jiang makes his way to the camper with the others close behind. Once in, Ben thinks locking the camper door is a good idea. The rest of the friends agree. The sliding door closes, separating them from the damp outer world. This place smells of licorice and friends. Once inside the safety of the van, Yanu says "The keys are missing." "What happened?" Sophia asks. "Where the keys used to be, there are streaks of mud," Yanu answers. Katie adds, "The mud is on the screen too! It's ripped open."

Back at the store, Yanu's Uncle picks up a baseball bat. Jiang's Father asks to borrow one of the store's walking sticks.

Both men cautiously step into the hallway toward the parent's bedroom. They listen intently for any sound coming from the empty room, or anywhere in the house. They turn quietly into the bedroom. They feel the breeze from the open window. They both look in that direction. They see the screen has been torn away. They peer around corners and look under the bed for the creature that may have entered. Nothing is found under the bed. The corners of the room and closets are undisturbed. They turn slowly to approach the window. Yanu's Uncle notices the mud-streaked dresser top. A perfume bottle and photograph are knocked over. Jiang's Father carefully steps toward the window and looks out. He gasps and takes a step back. "Look," he says to Yanu's Uncle. With fear on their faces, they look through the torn screen. They glance from side to side, taking in the area outside. There are several huge, deep, human-like footprints visible.

One set with toes facing the window. One set with toes pointing away. The adults now understand the danger is not within the house. What reached through the window took what it wanted, then left. Yanu's Uncle slams the window shut and locks it. He hangs the CLOSED sign in the store window and leaves with haste. A nervous sense of electricity is felt by everyone as they watch the two grown men run toward the camper.

Chapter 7

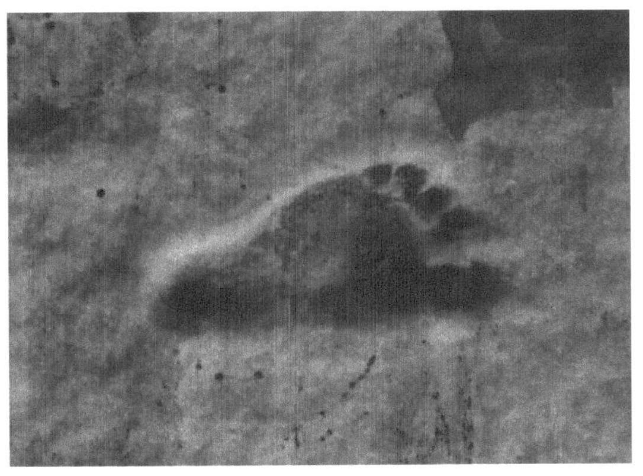

Back at the town meeting, the door swings open. A whooshing sound is barely heard above the murmur and rustle of papers. Few people notice the large woman with red hair making her way into the back of the room. She slides her chair out slowly and settles down. The folding chair groans as the thin metal legs support her weight. A few people sitting close to her are made uneasy by her heavy jasmine perfume. The man from the local government speaks, he states zoo entry is a matter of public safety. There have been reports of damage to a nearby farm. Wild animal paw and hoof prints were found in a demolished pumpkin field.

Lucas' Father is the next person to speak. He explains to them this newly discovered endangered species must be protected. The mouse he brought is no ordinary mouse. The zoo must be declared a sanctuary for this special creature. The last speaker reads the deed. It states that the rightful owner of the zoo is listed as M. Yeren. The last day the zoo was open was one year and nine months ago. The property taxes are paid. This zoo is still considered private property. No one can enter the zoo without permission from the owner.

The local government agrees with the townspeople to uphold public safety. They promise to also consider the possibility of an endangered species living in the zoo. Jiang's Mom shares photos from her SD card. She explains that the pictures were retrieved from the drone after it flew over the zoo. The drone was later found wrecked, lying outside of the zoo wall. She shows pictures of an animal's tongue, a dog's nose, and large teeth. The towns-people and officials agree the zoo must be studied. They end the meeting with a plan to fly another drone. This time the drone must obey the no trespassing law. It must fly four hundred feet above the zoo.

As the meeting ends, the large red headed woman in the back row gets up from her chair. She leaves a trail of jas-mine perfume. The sound of something metal rattles inside her purse.

The adults drive home from the town meeting. At the same time, the camper is making its way down the bumpy mountain road back to Jiang's house. When the friends arrive, Jiang's Father and sends them to the playroom downstairs. In the middle of the room is an old ping- pong ta-ble. The girls sit in a circle near the table on the blue carpeted floor. Ben, Lucas and

Jiang listen, as they reach for the pad-
dles.

Yanu and Katie share the details of
what they saw in the bedroom. The torn
screen, the streaks of mud on the ran-
sacked dresser top. The boys hear part of
the conversation. The small white ball
bounces back and forth on the bright green
table.

The adult voices talking on phones can
be heard in the background. After a few
rounds of ping-pong, curiosity about another game takes over. They open their
phones to the zoo game. They do their
best to beat the monster who keeps taking
the keys. The longer they keep the keys
from the large, hairy humanoid-ape, the
higher the score. Jiang's Mother returns
from the town meeting. She is surprised to
see Yanu's Uncle. The men explain what
happened at the hiker's country store. A
few minutes later, the local police call
Yanu's Uncle. They are ready to meet him

at the store. Jiang's Father takes Yanu and her uncle back up the hill. As he is driving, she turns around to see her parents' yellow car through the back window. They are returning from that town meeting. Behind their car, a police car can be seen. Yanu is thinking, "This is beyond weird."

Jiang's Father parks the car. He gives his statement to the police as a witness. They take his phone number. They say that he may return home. Yanu's family gives their statement to the police officers. They open the store and cautiously enter to retrieve pictures taken by the security camera. Yanu's family reports a set of keys as the only missing object. When the police ask; "Keys to what?" Her father confirms no one is sure what lock they open. The police officers look confused. They begin taking notes. Yanu's Mother speaks up. She adds that the keys were found by her husband while cleaning the rain gutter. The police officers have a look of concern.

They go through the house as a precaution.

The police take pictures of the mud-streaked dresser top, the torn screen, and the footprints outside of the window. Yanu's Uncle confirms that he was the one who shut and locked the window. Then they review the security camera photos. The pictures show a dark circle of a face peering into the camera. It is out of focus. They see photos of a few birds. There is a photo after dark of a coyote sniffing the store doorway. The last two photos are the most alarming. The time and date stamps show they were taken just before the town hall meeting today. One picture is blurry. It shows a furry, reddish, figure walking to-ward their store. The last one is the same tall, hairy, unfocused figure walking away. It is barely visible disappearing into the tree line in the woods behind their home.

Chapter 8

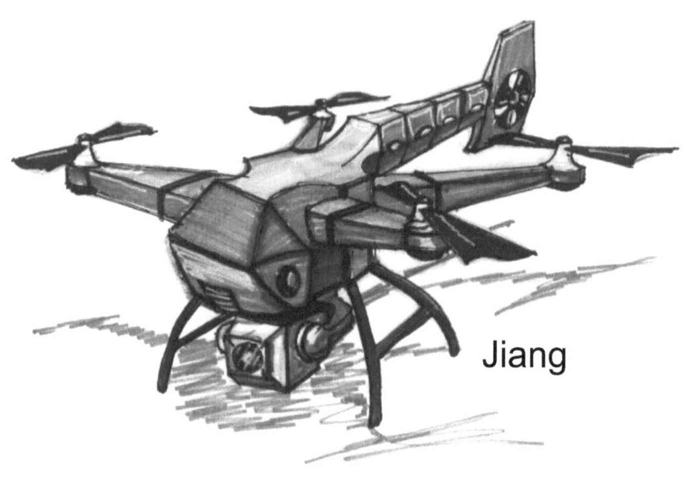

It is a mid-June day. Lucas hopes he gets a text from Jiang. Everyone has been waiting for the arrival of the remote-controlled aircraft. Lucas' Father is working in the garage. His mouse Kingston is curled up, sleeping in his bedding. Lucas walks into his father's room. On his father's desk is a large, rolled-up poster. Lucas wonders what it may be. He sits on the chair and unrolls the stiff paper. On the large, glossy photo is a picture of HIS mouse. Lucas realizes this is what his fa-ther took to that show and tell town meeting. The words read; "Pacific Pocket Mouse." The smaller print explains how this mouse is protected by the endangered species act of 1994. It helps maintain plant diversity. There are only 150 left in existence. Lucas is thinking that this means his mouse is important. Lucas goes on to read; "The US marines have a legal requirement. Their operations must be conducted in a way that respects the Pocket Mouse's environment."

"Kingston IS like royalty." He smiles to himself. Suddenly, Lucas' phone vibrates. It is Jiang letting him know that his parent's quadcopter has arrived. Lucas does his best to roll the poster back the way he found it. He hopes his father can take him to Jiang's.

The friends all manage to make it to Jiang's yard. Ben reminds them to stay four hundred feet in the air above the zoo. Katie and Sophia are sharing ideas about what will be photographed. They remember the photo of a shadowy zoo creature that was watching from behind tree branches. The drone hums, it rises. It crosses the farmer's blossoming pumpkin field. It crosses over the stream, the storm drain, the zoo wall. They are careful to avoid tree branches. Jiang's Parents keep the flight simple. They hover over the largest clearing. Then they slowly circle around the zoo boundary. The drone hovers once more over the center of the zoo. Then, it makes its way back to them. It flies over the stream. The buzzing can be heard as it approaches them. It crosses the farmer's field. Dogs bark in the distance.

The humming of Jiang's drone had awakened the Forest Zoo's inhabitants. The animals remember this bug flew over the zoo before. It was that epic fall night. Claire the hog showed Tiger the place she was born. They ran wild and gobbled amazing food in the open field. The same plants from the field seemed to have followed them to this place. They remember the trip through the zoo's storm drain. That passage led to a night of food discovery and tasty seeds everywhere. The water washed away any evidence of paw and hoof prints from the storm drain. Now the zoo smells like the farmer's field. The big, weird buzzing bug is back. The zoo animals take cover in the trees. The sound abruptly stops. They cautiously resume searching for food, and swimming in the stream.

Jiang's family and his friends are watching the sky. THWAAT! This sound silences the hum of the drone. A hawk's brown wings and red tail are visible as it strikes the flying object. This is followed by the abrupt descent of the drone into the field below. The friends look at each other. Jiang's parents agree to carefully cross the field to retrieve the downed aerial photographer. Gwen, Lucas, and Jiang assure the parents that everyone will play safely in the yard. The friends watch the parents carefully crossing the pumpkin patch. Jiang's Parents take care not to step on the blossoms. These flowers will later become the farmer's gourds. They find the downed drone stuck halfway into the soil. The black, silent piece of technology looks small in this wide-open field. They both breathe a sigh of relief. They see the small camera is still securely attached. Trying to retrace their steps, they make their way back to the house. The friends run to the edge of the field to meet them. "Can we see? What happened?"

They swarm around the two adults holding onto the device. "We must see if the pictures are saved," Jiang's mom explains. The kitchen table serves as the place for removing the SD card from the drone's camera. The card is retrieved. Jiang's parents insert the camera card into the computer slot. It seems to take forever to load.

The small images appear slowly on the computer screen. Everyone crowds in to see the zoo photos taken from the air. The first image shows muddy, pink back legs, and a curly tail. It looks like a pig rooting near the bushes in the stream.

The next image is what Sophia and Katie have been waiting to see all along. It is the face that was the circle from Jiang's photo. That circle of a head. The curled stick can be seen as a tail rising up behind that head. The head has a face with wide eyes that are staring curiously at the camera. This is a monkey's face. The brown hands are grasping a tree branch.

The next image shows an animal with long white fur. It is the size of a large dog. It is in the center of scattered debris next to a small building. It is hard to see what kind of animal it is as its head is buried in bits of paper.

The next picture shows a large dog with black and white markings, like a cow. It appears to be looking up at the camera and barking. The next few photos show small buildings with fading paint. Surrounding these small buildings are exactly the SAME pumpkin blossoms that now fill the farmer's field. Lucas points at the picture. "My father told me our mouse helps with mixing different kinds of seeds. Maybe those are from the seeds my mouse planted."

The other children look to Sophia as she nods in agreement. She feels a bit of pride. She gave that mouse his first ride in her bicycle basket. The next picture is by rocks and a stream. They gasp as they see a tiger crouching, looking warily up at the camera. It has a broad face and gold eyes. Its black stripes separate the orange and white fur in its coat. At once the group understands. This may be the source of the wild animal paw prints left in the farmer's field. "Maybe there are more ti-gers?" suggests Gwen. They search the rest of the photos. They find only vegetation, and small buildings. The next photo shows the open talons and spread wings of the hawk. The next picture is the sky. The last photo is the camera's landing place on the brown and green earth.

Chapter 9

The friends are up to level fifty in the Forest Zoo game. They agree to meet at Lucas' place. Lucas' Father sets up a picnic table by the bird feeder. This is the designated *chill place* for today. According to the game rules, getting the key to the gate will open it. Opening the gate guarantees ownership of the Forest Zoo. Another player joins the game. No one knows who it is. The new player's avatar is a small monkey. Whoever is controlling the monkey is catching up quickly. Winning the desired set of keys in the game just got more complicated. Lucas and Yanu think this game knows too much. The rest of the friends agree. They also agree the wrong person cannot win the game and get the keys to the gate and open it.

Gwen remembers the superpower bond the friends share. She thinks, "What would a ninja do?" She suggests that they all tap into their skills. They want to outsmart the new opponent. Yanu understands everything leaves tracks. The maker of the game has included all of the forest zoo animals. Katie notices no previous scores for highest player. That means the game hadn't been played until Katie and Sophia opened the link on the zoo's website.

Sophia wants to use her superpower as a fairy princess. The mouse, Kingston, has special recognition. It works the same as royalty. The mouse must have a rightful claim to the zoo keys. The zoo was Kingston's habitat. Lucas remembers his mouse attending a meeting. Mice don't usually attend meetings. Maybe there is something to Sophia's royalty idea. Ben wonders; "What would a cowboy do?" Ben remembers watching the movies at his aunt's house. The Lone Ranger would form a posse. The only people he could think of were some of the other kids from the playground. Ben had wanted to meet a few of them. Since they were older, he didn't know how to approach them. Some of the older kids used the playground to flex. It was hard to get "in".

An anonymous invitation to the game may be a start. They won't know where it came from. Ben asks Sophia if she can write the game link on the restaurant's dry erase board. Sophia agrees. She picks a weekend. The adults will be too busy to notice the change. While Ben and Sophia work on adding members to the game, Jiang studies the zoo photos. Jiang thinks the pictures show animals doing just fine without people. His next thought is; "If we win the game, we should throw the keys to the zoo away." Jiang goes to the computer and hits the share button. He sends the aerial zoo photos retrieved from the drone to his friends. He then watches his parents repair the drone. The damage is mostly dirt clean up. Luckily, after colliding with the hawk, the drone fell to the soft earth.

The more the friends study the photos Jiang sent, the stronger their skills get. Each person from the group sees something the other person can't. Lucas and Sophia notice the pumpkin plants in the new zoo photos, but none in the old website photos. Gwen's ninja brain is trying to figure out the weakness in the wall. There had to be someplace in the zoo where the large animals made their way out. Yanu is remembering paw prints and destruction in the farmers' field. The animals were able to return quickly, and quietly. The farmer reported the prints stopped at the creek. Katie notices no one had been playing the game until and she and Sophia clicked on the link from the zoo website.

While playing the game, the friends notice a pattern that helps them score. The appearance of Yeren is based on the number of times each virtual zoo animal has contact with the keys. They keep track of the numbers. They find the possible solution to the game puzzle. The goal is to outsmart the large hairy bandit. While meeting in Jiang's game room, they form a strategy. The plan is to keep their avatars in a closed circle. In the game, they will pass the keys only to each other. The players must move only in the direction of the gate.

The friends work on their gaming skills during summer, and through early fall. By December, their scores seem high enough for the ultimate game. The strategy is to work together as a group. The game's design is to rack up points by working as a team, and moving toward the gate. The whole time they had been sitting next to each other, they were competing with each other. Their hope now is to work together to keep control of the keys. Jiang reminds them that his mother had been talking with his dad after the town hall meeting. There was some connection with the holder of the keys, and zoo ownership. Maybe winning them in a game would win them in real life. Yanu thinks getting the keys back is crucial. She remembers finding them when her father cleaned the gutter. It felt wrong to have them taken from her parent's bedroom. All of her friends were just as determined to win them back for their own reasons.

Chapter 10

Ninja Gwen

Suddenly everyone is talking about some virus. It is a sickness is worse than the flu. The news is shocking. This can't be real. Exactly this weekend the playgrounds are shut down due to the pandemic. Social distancing and masks are a requirement. Sophia's parents convert their play area behind the restaurant for outdoor seating. Ben and Lucas text the plan to begin playing at 11am on Saturday. Sophia sent a text back, *FOMO! I have a Zoom music lesson that morning. Is 7pm better?* Lucas shares her text with the group. Everyone confirms that 7pm is better. No one was excited to think about their Saturday morning jobs at home. The friends all know they have a strategy. Working together is so important. The new requirement to wear masks and shelter in place is changing everything. This Saturday has them all separated. With each friend in a separate location, knowing the teammates' avatar is crucial.

The group text goes out about the game; *Secure your hotspot. Know your friends*. This Saturday morning is keeping everyone on edge. They grind through their work and keep their phones close.

Saturday at six Ben gets all of his homework done early. He puts out a tweet: *#LetsGetToIt*. Coming from Ben, they know what that means. He wants to get a jump on the game before everyone else figures out that this day is special. Ben and Sophia posted the game website at the restaurant. The new players give their players a higher status. The "noob" crowd has been keeping the game primate busy. So far, no one has been able to keep the keys away from the Yeren long enough to make it to the gate. The team signs on. They notice that one avatar is missing; Gwen's ninja. Yanu sends a text. Gwen, what's up? Gwen sends a message back. *Streaming is SLOW. Mom's remote learning lesson plan is big*. Gwen does not want to be the reason the plan unravels. Yanu sends a message back. *Shop closing early. Streaming strong here*.

Gwen thinks quickly. She calls out, "Mom, we are out of bread. Can I get some?" Her mom, focused on her lesson, answers back. "Just get some from Sophia's and get right back." Gwen knows that she better come back with some bread. Sophia's restaurant is just down the well-lit street very close to their home. Her mom doesn't know that the bread at Sophia's sells out by evening. Gwen's Mother also doesn't know about this big game night. The streaming at the restaurant may be too slow for the game. Sophia's is not her first choice.

Gwen knows that Yanu had invited her. Her store always has bread. It has been dark for about an hour now. Gwen is thinking that if she takes the shortcut, she can get directly to Yanu's place. Maybe she can get a ride back home. Her family has always been nice. Gwen hopes that she is making the right choice. She answers "Okay mom." She sends Yanu a text: *I'll be at your place in 15 min*. She grabs money from the counter. She puts on her jacket and out the door she goes. Gwen takes her bicycle to make up in time what she has to do in distance. Ninja rules do not apply in the woods. At night, being small and quiet is not a good choice for humans. Stealth and silence are the tools of bobcats, and coyotes. People have been known to startle bears that are not hibernating yet. When they took a field trip to the State Park the forest ranger spoke to the class. His instructions come back to Gwen clearly. The best bobcat and coyote defense is to stay together, look big, and make a lot of noise. The rule for being anywhere near a bear is to leave quickly and quietly by retracing your steps.

Gwen approaches the shortcut from her house. Her bicycle tires make crunching and popping sounds on the cold gravel. Not being in a group feels scary. She pushes away from the safety of her well-lit home into the darkness. She hopes her puffy coat and hat make her look bigger. She gathers her courage. The only noise that she can make now is her voice. She turns on her bike light. Gwen knows that singing is the simplest way to be loud. The last time that she sang anything was while babysitting. Most wild animals prefer not to mess with humans. Making noise is good.

She takes a deep breath. To her surprise, the words come out. "I am just a bobcat, scratching on a tree. All you creepy night things, nothing here to see. Bang! bang! biggity-ding, dang-a-dang!" Her song hangs as steam in the air. Her laughter makes more steam. Humor seems, for the moment, to replace her fear.

Yanu's text, *see you soon*, vibrates unnoticed in Gwen's backpack. Gwen keeps her focus and continues to sing while pedaling. Her bike light bounces off of some potholes and dirt. Gwen takes a breath. In that moment of quiet, she can hear a twig snap behind her. She has come too far to go back. She belts out another verse and pedals faster. Her bouncing bike light reveals the last curve in the road. A dim light shines on a small porch, and log benches. This hiker's country store is a welcome sight. Gwen takes a quick look over her shoulder. The cold air strikes her cheekbone. Her eyes search the place from where she had come. She sees nothing in the darkness.

Flipping her head back, Gwen stands on her bike pedal. Pressing down with her full weight provides leverage. She crosses the parking lot quickly, and pulls up to the front step. With her hat sliding over one eye, she steps up and reaches for the door handle. She can see the top of a dark head of hair through the glass. She pushes the door open, half dragging her bicycle across the doorway. Yanu's startled mother almost trips over her mask display. Gwen, full of energy and without an explanation simply says, "Hello!" The look of surprise is replaced with a concerned smile from Yanu's mom. "Where did you come from?" "My Mom sent me for bread. Is Yanu home?" Gwen knows full well that her friend is waiting for her to join her in the game. Yanu's mother answers "Oh, you are lucky, we have a few loaves left. Yes, Yanu is home." Right on cue, the back door to the store opens, revealing her friend's welcome face. With pretend surprise, Gwen greets her. Gwen brings her bike into the store. She carefully leans it against a corner wall. She lays the money for the bread on the counter. With just a smile and no further explanation, the two head upstairs. Yanu's mom continues to prepare the store for closing.

The girls run down the hallway and upstairs to her room. They both open their phones to the game and sit on the floor. They join the game that has been going on for 45 minutes. Before Gwen arrived, Yanu's tracker avatar had been paying attention to the marks Yeren left after showing up in the game. There are little shadows left on the ground. Katie had explained to everyone that the primate would not show up in the game in the same place twice. Yanu reminds Gwen what Katie said. Gwen's ninja avatar still has a strong position. Knowing where to put her player is paramount.

Lucas, Katie, Sophia, Jiang and Ben breathe a sigh of relief as Gwen's player shows up. The friends team up and form a circle. They move their avatars close to the gate. The keys are tossed from player to player while moving through the virtual zoo. Just as the keys are mid-air, the unwelcome primate arrives. Everyone knows she will grab the keys, and then quickly disappear. Jiang's drone player acts as a tank. He hovers and darts and distracts Yeren. Sophia's fairy princess character uses music that shows up in the game as sound waves. The sound waves seem to confuse Yeren. The primate moves back. Gwen's ninja springs into a front flip, intersecting with the keys that had been hanging mid-air. As her player lands on the ground, Lucas' zookeeper steps in and takes them. His player can move sideways. That is the right direction of the gate.

Hacker Katie   Cowboy Ben

Yeren moves forward again. Ben's cowboy tosses a lasso. It catches Yeren's arm. Katie's player is standing at the gate. Lucas moves one more time. The keys are passed. Katie's powers in the game are strategy and manual dexterity. She suc-ceeds in placing the keys into the zoo's locked gate. With a swipe of her arm Yeren swats the drone. It crashes. With her lassoed arm, she tosses Ben's cowboy into the air. As the zoos' gate swings open, all motion in the game stops. The solid white letters G.G. appear on the screen.

Stunned, Yanu and Gwen turn their heads, with mouths half-open, they smile. Jiang is home, holding his phone, looking at his player as a crashed drone on a frozen screen. "Good game?" He says out loud. A moment later Yanu's bedroom door swings open. Yanu's mother speaks gently, but firmly, "Girls, it is too late to be out riding a bike. We will take Gwen home." Gwen realizes that she better answer the text from her mom. She is relieved to see that it was just sent a few minutes ago. Gwen answers back, *On my way*. The girls quickly put on their coats, and pass through the now closed store. Gwen sweeps her gaze shyly looking for her excuse to be there. The neatly wrapped loaf of bread is lying on the glass counter with her change. Thanking Yanu's mom, she scoops them off of the counter and rushes out.

The cool air hits her face as she makes her way out into the dark. She joins Yanu. Her bike is already loaded into the back of their van. Gwen is grateful, embarrassed, and excited all at the same time. The girls click their seat belts on and ride silently back to Gwen's. She does not want her mother to see the headlights. A half-block from her house Gwen offers "Maybe you can park here?" With luck, there is a place to pull over before the driveway. A large bush blocks the headlights. Gwen jumps out. It feels like forever as Yanu's father lifts her bike from the back. "Thank you!" Gwen says and pushes her bike past the bush and up her driveway. They step out and watch her enter the small door next to the garage. The door closes. The light in the garage shows through the glass panel.

Yanu's parents get back into the van. Before driving away, Yanu shows her parents the text from Gwen: *Safely home*.

Chapter 11

December days at the Forest Zoo are not quite as fun as the long summer days. Bhatan the tiger is finding less fish and frogs in the stream. Shu and his family barely budge from their log. They would make a tasty treat for a tiger, or even a dog. Kingston's cousins are tucked away in a discarded cardboard box. They feel safe with their seeds in their unseen corner of the gift shop.

Capu the monkey's brown fur is thick now. Her friend Glad Goat's white fur is full and bushy. The white fur has some broken twigs tangled in places too hard to reach. The remnants of crushed pumpkins on the ground are becoming scarce. Claire the hog and Speckle Dog are rooting near the zoo's storm drain. They sniff the air. Claire knows the scent of the forbidden and exciting farm. Claire can see the tiger is catching less fish. She knows a trip through the storm drain for food will soon be necessary.

The tiger has never been interested in chasing his friends as food. Before escaping his cage, he caught fish from the stream that ran through his enclosure. It was better than what came from Capu. She would wrestle open peanut butter jars, then playfully toss them through the bars. Now that Bhatan is free, he notices that the others smell like the peanut butter. Fish and frogs seem tastier.

The neighborhood friends are feeling the same strain. They all feel the isolation of winter and the social distancing. Ben already knows how to "cowboy up". Being wise and ready was not new to most of them. The wisdom seems to be in knowing who to call.

After winning the game, it remains frozen and not playable. Everyone has shifted their focus to remote learning. A week passes by. The winter maintenance starts early at the country store. This morning Yanu sweeps a light snow from the steps. Her broom hits a small rock. The soft bristles do not move the rock. Frustrated, she moves in to get a closer look at the obstacle. It is a dark clump of ice stuck to the stone step. With the broom's stick end, she nudges at its edges. It still doesn't budge. Yanu now leans on the object. This pressure propels the obstacle up into the air. It lands, leaving two dark circles in the snow. She takes two steps down to investigate.

With the broom handle, she pokes. The dirt is nothing more than that, dirt. She checks the other circle in the snow. Something slides away with each poke of the broom handle. Impatiently, she reaches. Through her mitten she feels a familiar object. With unbelievable excitement, she thinks, "the keys!" With joy, she scoops them up.

Yanu runs to the store, spreading the news. She explains to her parents that she found the keys on the step. They had been caked in mud, ice and snow. It is just before the store's opening time. Wearing coats and boots, the family thoroughly examines the entire parking lot. They check the wooded area surrounding the house. Yanu and her parents see no signs of tracks or footprints. They place the keys into an envelope. The envelope is placed under the cash register drawer. They open their store with plans to check the security cameras later.

In the meantime, Yanu sends a group text, *I found the keys*. This text shifts their focus from remote learning, back to the zoo. Distracted, Lucas gets up to get a snack. He passes by his father's open laptop. He reads the headline news from the *Peninsula Review: S.U. receives donation of land. State University announced Wednesday that it has accepted a donation of a thirty-acre parcel formerly known as The Forest Zoo. This parcel spans wetlands, and forests of fir and cedar. It also harbors one of the most endangered species in the nation: the Pacific Pocket Mouse. The University plans to maintain the landscape as a living place of water conservation, forest management, insect, plant, wildlife and ecology. The property was donated by M. Yeren.*

"Dad!" Lucas calls out, running into the kitchen. "We won the keys to the zoo in a game. Yanu actually found the keys! Can a university own a zoo?"

Chapter 12

The official preparation for the zoo entry begins. The photos of the zoo taken by Jiang's drone were shared with the group. Lucas shared them with his father. His father sends them to the university. In the subject line, he writes, *Safety concern regarding the zoo's inhabitants*. A polite email response is received from the Dean's office. It confirms his concern regarding safety.

The University finds Yanu's Father has been listed as the zoo's trustee. The legal documents state the transfer of the keys must occur from the trustee before the property belongs to the University. The friends all know it's about them winning the game. They were the ones who unlocked the virtual zoo gate. Yanu's Parents seem to have been given the keys TWICE. Yanu's Parents receive written notification from the school. They accept the duty of trustees.

This new responsibility creates a family discussion. Yanu suggests feeding the animals. Her parents are concerned that she may try it. They hold onto the keys. They agree on a plan for her to throw food over the zoo wall. The next day they load the van with boxes of potatoes, dog food, corn, and fruit. Yanu and her father drive to the zoo's entrance and park. He is considering the best approach. Yanu asks her father, "Can we see if the keys match the old gate?" The keys are secured in the glove box. Her father answers, "It will be safer to feed them over the wall." Relieved, they see an SUV show up with a university logo. There is a rack on the roof with a ladder. Two large men and a woman step out of the vehicle. They unload large containers of meat, corn, squash, potatoes and baskets of fruit. Yanu and her father walk over and introduce themselves. They all agree on the importance of providing food during the winter.

Without hesitation, the crew gets down to business. The zoo gate remains locked. They prop a ladder against the 16-foot wall. First, one man climbs the ladder with a hook and rope. He is followed by another carrying a large container. The woman is holding the bottom of the ladder. The container with the tiger food is gently lifted to the man with the hook. Carefully, he fastens the container to the rope. He cautiously eases the food container over the zoo wall. The rope abruptly jerks. The sudden loss of weight nearly knocks the men off of the ladder. "I think we found the tiger," the woman holding the ladder says with amazement. Yanu's father realizes the food that he had in his car was not enough, but it is something. He approaches the officials. He asks them if he could toss some over the wall in a different area. Some animal behind the wall seems to be very hungry. The fruit, potatoes and dog food may be good for the other animals.

The officials agreed that spreading the food around in different areas is also wise. The animals may fight over food if fed in just one place.

On the side of the zoo by the drain, the hog, goat and dog are root grubbing. A monkey screech echoes in the stone passageway. This startles them. They lift their noses from the ground, sniffing the air. Capu had witnessed the tiger devouring food dropped over the wall. Capu now swings from treetops as she approaches. With muddy noses and perked ears, they leave the storm drain and run toward their friend. As they are running, they are met with an object falling aimlessly. It lands with a soft thud onto the forest floor a few feet ahead of them. All of them rush to investigate. Speckle is first to reach the morsel. With one sniff, and a gulp, it is gone. The others smell the remnants of food. The excitement peaks. Claire knows what this means. The farm has come to them.

On the other side of the wall, Yanu is handing her father pieces of animal food. He places the next soft, ripe apple in a dog toy launcher and throws it over the wall. Up, over and down. This is retrieved by the monkey before it hits the ground. She carries it away from the others, and up into a tree. It isn't long before the hog, dog, goat and pig see more food drop from the sky. This goes on until the rest of the food is emptied from the boxes.

Yanu and her father return to their van. Looking over at the school's SUV, Yanu's Father reaches into the glove box and retrieves the keys. He steps out and walks over to them as they approach their vehicle. Through the passenger window Yanu watches her father hand over the keys, the tool for entry to the Forest Zoo. As he gets back into the van, Yanu asks, "What if they don't work?" Her father answers, "I told them I never tried them. That way, if something is wrong in the Zoo, we won't be blamed" This makes sense to Yanu. Staying out of trouble is the best way to go.

Full of food, the animals go back to their little houses to sleep. The hog knows where there is food like this, there are people. The animals all know, after food, there is sleep.

Brisk, heavy crunching on the frozen ground awakens the tiger. Hearing this, Bhatan opens one eye. He doesn't change his breathing. He watches something huge walk away from him, through the zoo. He holds perfectly still. The figure fades into the tree line beyond the little houses.

Fed animals are easier to manage. The school Zoologists plan their next visit. The next morning, the sound of an engine stirs the monkey from her sleep. She springs out of the cedar tree and onto the top of the forest zoo wall. A shiny object catches her attention. It is the morning sun glistening on metal. It is the same SUV that was at the gate the day before. She screeches and jumps to the ground to wake the others. She bounces, chattering from little house to little house waking her friends. The dog, hog, goat, and tiger stand together in the December chill. They shake the cold from their fur, and wait for the next thing to happen. The locked gate slowly creaks open. They can see the three humans enter. They are wearing helmets, and carrying sacks and sticks. The animals cautiously observe the movement of the people. Their ears are twitching and upright, their nostrils are flared. Claire remembers as a piglet running from the human place. Bhatan has a long distrust of being fed by others. Remnants of his rusted cage are still visible on the ground. The smell of man's food is a trap. At once, curiosity is replaced by fear. The tiger moves first. He bolts for the safe and familiar stream. Then Claire and Speckle follow in a brisk trot. The stream leading to the storm drain *is* their way out. Bhatan makes it to the stone tunnel. Speckle and Claire are now in a full run. Capu questions the safety of the trees. She springs onto the ground. She feels safer joining her friends.

The splatter of wet feet, water and fur form a blur as the monkey tries to catch up. She doesn't notice that the goat is not behind her. The light is getting brighter as she sees Claire's tail. Next, she sees the dog's hind legs. The tiger's haunches become visible. Then, the air in the tunnel changes. The cool moisture carries the distant smell of the farm.

Back at the zoo, while nibbling paper, Glad Goat does not see danger. He just sees what he wants. The people with the apples seem nice enough. His friends are always acting crazy. The men and women in hats pat him on the head, and brush a few tangles from his fur. They drop more apples, then some corn cobs. Startled by something, the people look up. They are watching the trees. Their attention is drawn to something. The goat is focused on eating as they slowly walk away.

The Zoologists continue to search everything. The quest for the endangered species has so far resulted in one goat. They make their way to the abandoned zoo gift shop. The rusted door lock gives way easily. Once inside they get the validation they were searching for. The discovery of Kingston's cousins snuggled in the gift shop is epic. The family of pocket mice gets legendary treatment. Their box is gently lifted into a bigger box. They are carried from the zoo's broken gift shop.

Shu's pointed whiskered nose is barely visible. He watches intently. His family is snuggled under their log. They cautiously watch with brown eyes. They are not noticed by the men. Shu watches the procession of boots. The men in hats walk by carrying boxes.

Chapter 13

The animals exit through the storm drain is easy. Where to go on the other side? This question causes the blood to rush from their hearts to their legs. They feel energetic from having eaten well. This allows them to decide with their minds and not their stomachs. The sun is up. Instinct tells them this is the wrong time to be walking out in the open. Claire is the first to step down from the tunnel. She places her hooves carefully onto the rocks. She then makes her way down to the edge of the forest. Capu, not wanting to be left out, jumps next. Speckle follows.

Bhatan stays behind. He carefully surveys the open field that leads to the farm. Everything looks so different from the night that he and the hog hunted. His memory shows it full of orange globes and tasty treats. Now the field is dried vines and furrowed bare ground. The tiger doesn't see the goat. Everyone else is missing as well. They must have gone into the trees. Bhatan, with one great leap, lands onto the rocks. With one more lunge, he enters the woods.

Shu notices the quiet in the zoo. His whiskered nose sniffs the air. There is no scary smell of the giant cat, or that big, fast, long-legged dog. Shu's lean brown body stretches out into the forest sunlight. Turning back quickly, he looks for his family members. One by one, they pop out from under the log. All six of them become visible. It feels good to stretch. The space under the log is safe, but dark and small. This winter air is different. It carries the smell of apples, corn, and a goat. The goat smell is not a threat to them. The food must have come from the men that walked through. The Shu family joins the goat. They eat corn and apples from the ground. After sharing the goat's food, Shu's body is somewhat round. He knows that staying out in the open too long may invite hawks. The family leaves as quickly as they came. Shu is the last one under their log home. He has some trouble fitting.

The activity at the zoo does not go un-noticed. Yanu's parents confirm the University is feeding the animals. The paperwork as trustees is completed. The keys are handed over. Feeling responsible, as Kingston is their celebrity, Sophia, Lucas and their friends continue to watch the zoo. They all know Jiang's place has a clear view of the stream and storm drain. Students interact in real life within a specified group. The school refers to these groups as bubbles. In the bubble, Katie's old feeling of being the "new kid" vanishes. She is recognized. The swab shows that all members of her group are negative. There is a Covid positive family. They have their own group and friends. Masks become a part of all activities outside of the bubble. Jiang knows that his parents wear face shields and special masks at work. When they come home from work, there are marks on his parent's faces. These marks fade by morning. The lines around their mouths remind him of Halloween night. His mask had been on too tight. His mask left little lines as well. These lines faded quickly from around his eyes.

The house rules are: Shoes are to be placed on a rack by the door. Wash your hands for 20 seconds after being outside. Grocery bags are placed on a separate table. The items are sorted and cleaned. Fruits and vegetables get washed with special soap made for vegetables. All of the other items are sprayed with 70% alcohol. No mask means no going outside. The kid's masks are softer than Jiang's Parent's masks. Yanu's store got some cool ones in. Sometimes the stores don't have enough. Not wanting to depend on an outside source, Gwen has the urge to try to make her own. She streams videos to get some ideas. Her mother's sewing machine is just sitting in the spare room. Gwen asks if she can use it. After a few safety lessons, she is given permission to operate the machine. She manages to make a halfway decent mask. Then she makes two more. Sewing becomes less scary the more that she does it.

Lucas' Dad tells him his mom's project in Alaska is put on hold. After testing negative, she can fly home. On the day of her flight, Lucas and his dad drive their dark green truck to the airport. A woman who looks like she could be his mom's sister is waiting for them at the airport curb. The vehicle door swings open. Lucas sees this woman as she steps in. Her hair is longer than he remembers from the video conference. The boots that were new when she left for Alaska are now old and beat up. Lucas feels strange and happy as she hugs him. Lucas realizes everything is really different. Overnight, all the rules have changed. He hasn't decided if things are worse, or better. It seems like it is a mix of both. The friends focus on the new virtual classroom. To keep their friendships within the bubble, the playground friends move inside. Every weekend, Jiang's place is a perfect strategic location to watch the zoo. They decide to up their game with zoo supervision. With Lucas' Mom back, it feels more like a holiday. Lucas explains his biology lesson requires him to watch birds. She let him borrow his dad's binoculars. This will help with zoo watching tremendously. The next weekend, Lucas leaves his binoculars with Jiang for safe keeping.

Ben, Lucas and Jiang all share the fact that they don't have to worry if their socks match for virtual class. Sophia, Gwen and Yanu share how they hide a messy room from the teacher. They just shut the closet door. They change the angle of their computer screen to show a closed closet door behind them. Some kids hang posters up. Some have virtual backgrounds.

Yanu's store is busier than ever. With theaters shut down and the restrictions on restaurants, more and more people are hiking the trail. Her uncle is helping at the store. With the extra customers, her parents are more rushed than before. Now Yanu is the one feeling isolated. The weekend cannot come fast enough. On Saturday, the friends finally meet at Jiang's. Sophia and Gwen are close enough to ride to their friend's house. Yanu's Mother takes turns with Lucas' mother in picking up, and dropping off the rest of the group.

While at Jiang's, Sophia asks, "What's up with the zoo?" Lucas and Ben shrug. Gwen looks over at Yanu. Then everyone is looking at Yanu. This makes her shrug and look down at the floor shyly. "I just know that my father made sure the school was feeding the animals. He says the trucks with food show up every evening." The subject shifts to trying to keep up with the daily school lessons. They all admit that studying alone is a nightmare. Texting isn't always the best way to share information about lessons. While at Jiang's, the friends decide to form a study group. The parents agree that this may reduce the social separation problem. Gwen's house is midway between Sophia and Yanu's. Every weekday morning, Sophia and Yanu are dropped off at Gwen's house. Gwen's mother increases her streaming ability. The girls must obey the house rules. Study first, second, complete all assignments on time. On the other end of town, Ben, Jiang,

Lucas and Katie make their own study group. Lucas' chill place is now a study place. Lucas' mother enforces the same rules. They must prepare for class. They must show up for the video stream on time. The friends admit to each other the mixing of school with home life is strange. Everyone's home is now the bubble of safety.

Getting food at Sophia's now involves an app. If the outdoor dining area is full, most people get take out. Being outside is everything. Every park or place resembling a park is discovered by the people in the neighborhood. The other source of neighborhood fascination is the zoo. The University trucks are showing up for feedings. The debris they are hauling away has everyone curious. What is not shared to anyone by the school is that most of the zoo animals are not always IN the zoo.

Chapter 14

At dinner, Lucas' Father mentions the university article from the *Peninsula Review.* It is titled "Little Gardener." This article highlights the new University pocket mouse habitat. Right after dinner, Lucas opens the article on his phone. There are pictures of Kingston's pocket mouse family in their new habitat. The Forest Zoo progress is outlined next. It shows that care is taken not to upset the zoo's terrain. The article shows pictures. Lucas sees dried stalks of pumpkin, corn and tomato vines. They look wildly uneven on the half-frozen soil. The article states this vegetation growth is a clear example of what happens when nature is left on its own. Credit is given to the pocket mouse for carrying these seeds in his cheeks. The seeds are too big to be carried by the wind. The article mentions that the plants match the neighboring farm field. No record of agriculture was ever noted within the zoo. The article also shows the progress of the zoo cleanup. Pictures of the animals are shown. These photos are the same ones taken by Jiang's drone. Lucas wonders why there are no new animal photos in the zoo article. He sees his friend Kingston content in his bedding. He feels connected to activities in the zoo. He sends the link to his friend's phones.

That night Lucas gets some blurry picture texts from Jiang. They were taken with binoculars attached to his cell phone. When enlarged, you can see animals entering the zoo storm drain at sunset.

The school's work within the zoo continues. Each evening, they leave food in the zoo. They arrive cautiously every morning. The food containers are always empty. Hoof and paw prints are left scattered around the feeding areas. The only animal they ever find is the goat. No one from the University wants to work in the zoo at night. Only during daylight, the school workers repair and paint the little houses. They renovate the zoo's gift shop into an animal hospital.

It is January. The school year continues in its remote way. Jiang is getting ready for class. Last weekend, Yanu told her friends that the University has been leaving food for the zoo animals at night. The blurry picture Jiang sent to Lucas confirms this. The zoo animals have been avoiding the daytime workers. Jiang wonders if he will see the zoo animals leave. As Jiang waits for the photo opportunity, Yanu and her uncle make their way down the bumpy mountain road. In a clearing above the trees something is visible in the sky. Yanu sees a dark flying object. It looks like Jiang's drone. She sends him a text. *Hey, Is that your drone?* Jiang responds, *Where?* Yanu answers, *Up in the sky right now.* Jiang sets his laptop down and runs to the cabinet in the living room. He pulls the bottom drawer out quickly. To his relief, he sees the black propeller sticking out of brown paper. His parents wrapped it up after the hawk collision and repair. Jiang runs back to his phone to text, *Mine is home.* Yanu answers, *Someone else must have one.* It is almost time for class. Jiang's Parents have finished the night shift. After getting Jiang his breakfast, they went to bed. Lucas' mom is pulling up out front. Jiang stuffs his laptop into his backpack. He grabs his keys, coat and shoes and locks the door quietly.

The secret activities of the zoo inhabitants are not really a secret. The University now knows that the loose animals are THEIR problem. The friends always knew wild animals would occasionally show up in fields and forests. Now, once again, people are getting excited about it.

Speckle, Claire, Capu and Bhatan would leave the zoo through the storm drain just before daylight. The trip into the woods is a quick one. They avoid the men in hats every time. While out in the wild, the zoo friends adapt. Stay together, be alert. If the dark, buzzing man bug is heard, run for cover. Capu is now sitting in a fir tree. Claire, Speckle and Bhatan are snoozing in a bed of pine needles. Capu holds a branch with one hand. She is checking a twig for bugs with the other. There is no whirring sound from the sky. In fact, there are no sounds of wind, frogs or bugs. Everything is silent. Capu sees the dog's pointed ears move. Then Speckle stands up and is as still as the air. His gaze is set on a dark silhouette next to a large cedar tree. In the shadow, they can just see a massive, hairy figure. Capu screeches, Speckle growls, then barks, Claire moves from lying on her side, to bouncing up on all fours. Bhatan is now crouching. He is focused on the large vision standing still, watching them.

In one swift move, the figure darts into a shadow between two trees. Speckle's need to chase now takes over. His long legs easily move him to the place the tall visitor hid. The scent leads to a narrow crevice where two trees are intertwined. Capu stays in the high branches, screeching. Claire trots quickly. She hides behind a rock and watches. Speckle barks at this tree crevice. Bhatan runs up. With one forceful lunge, vanishes into the place between the two trees. Speckle stands at the tree base stunned. After taking a few steps back, he runs to the place of Bhatan's disappearance. He barks frantically. Dirt and moss fly as he scratches at the ground. Claire stands frozen behind her rock. Capu's commotion is interrupted by a menacing hum in the air.

Bhatan does not hear the chaos on the other side of the tree. His moment of darkness is replaced with a flash of light. Now he is standing in a familiar and calm place, the Forest Zoo. His friend, the goat trots towards him. This sight is strangely welcoming. The two greet each other with a few sniffs and a friendly head bump. Bhatan scans the zoo grounds. He sees men in hats visible by a distant building. They appear to be using sticks on the earth. The tiger does not want to attract the attention of the men. Bhatan's deep distrust of men makes him turn quietly away.

Glad Goat watches with curiosity. The tiger makes his way back down to the stream and tunnel. Bhatan approaches cautiously. He observes the pieces of metal stacked by the entrance. These things were not here when they left at dawn. Bhatan wastes no time getting into the tunnel. With large padded feet he splashes his way to the light at the other end.

OUT comes the huge tiger in the middle of the day. Bhatan nearly knocks over the large pieces of metal stacked on the other side. Feeling unsafe, he runs as quickly as he can back to where his friends are.

Claire sees Bhatan first. An excited squeal alerts Speckle and Capu. The noisy group of friends greets each other. They realize the zoo and the forest rules are changing. The tunnel can no longer be trusted. The forest is shared by things they don't understand.

Chapter 15

The school's drone photos never show anything but tree tops and local wildlife. There is no photographic proof of exotic animals outside of the zoo walls. Cameras mounted in trees inside the zoo have the most information. Just after dark, the cameras show animals arriving inside the zoo. They would sniff around before heading straight to the feeding containers. Then, they are photographed leaving before sunrise.

This information is important. They see the creek and storm drain as the animal trail. The school plans to build a metal grate. When the animals are inside for their nightly feeding, they plan to drop that metal grid over the tunnel entrance. The water in the stream will continue to flow freely. The exotic animals would have to stay inside the zoo. The men and women in hats examine the perimeter. They walk around the zoo's wall. The back of this 16-

foot wall facing the hillside is crumbling. There is a metal fence placed as a patch along the low spot. A member of the school staff notes a small piece of auburn fur tangled in the wire. They photograph the crumbling wall, and fence. With a stick, the reddish fur is pulled from the twisted metal. It is carefully wrapped up in a piece of paper. This sample will be sent to experts. They will identify what, or who it came from.

The school friends work away in their bubbles. Everyone is trying to follow the rules. Play with your safe friends. After dark, many people are off of the hiking trails. During the day, the school seems to be working intently on the storm drain. Jiang, Lucas and the rest of the group know why. This new life is involves playing backyard basketball, video classes and texting.

Claire, Capu, Speckle and Bhatan notice Glad Goat looking clean and happy.

The cages are gone. Their plants and dirt are still there. They were used to getting fish, tasty treats and their own globes when they are in season. The food from the men in hats is good as well. The woods are now a place where the large, hairy people disturb their sleep.

Bhatan remembers that metal things are being put up around their storm drain. Metal means cage. The animals walk over to the place the large hairy person stood. They examine the light shining through a crevice where the two trees are inter-twined. This is the place Bhatan jumped in-to, and then disappeared. The place he reappeared in the zoo may have the an-swer to coming and going whenever they want to. The storm drain may be blocked with metal. Figuring out the tree exit will let them come and go if they need to.

Capu, without notice jumps, runs, then dives into the crevice, then disappears. Speckle, Claire and Bhatan run from the forest with great excitement. They watch the tunnel entrance.

Capu sees darkness, then a flash of light. With a bounce, she lands on her feet. She is looking at the side of Claire's little house. It looks different in the daylight. The people must have made the door different. It is clean. She takes note of her point of entry. There is no intertwined tree like the one in the woods. How did she come through? She sprints toward the stream. She hops along the creek bed. The sunlight is glistening on something all around the tunnel entrance. This must be the cage. Cautiously, she jumps into the bushes next to the stream and listens. There is sound of rushing water. Edging slowly out, Capu peeks down the tunnel. The other end is still open. She RUNS in! Her hands and feet work in sync avoiding the cold water. The monkey propels herself toward the light. She feels the breeze on the fur of her face. Then OUT she springs, landing hard on the rocks next to where the water flows.

Capu can hear Speckle's loud and excited bark at the woods edge. She runs toward that sound. She enters the cover of trees, and is almost knocked over by Speckle and Claire. Bhatan is crouched nearby. His gold eyes blink. He understands.

Claire and Speckle are reluctant to lunge through the crevice to get back to the zoo. The zoo seems safer. Fear, for them, is its own cage. The group boldly trots out of the cover of the forest. They cross the field, climb the stones, and make their trek back through the tunnel. As they walk up the zoo's creek bed, they see Glad Goat standing near the water. He is looking past them. They look back to see several vehicles approaching the tunnel. The people in hats drop the metal grate over the storm drain entrance. When the grid is in place, the vehicles drive away.

Chapter 16

Katie, Jiang, Lucas and Ben are getting better with their study routine. Sophia, Yanu and Gwen are also no longer struggling with the new class schedule. It is February. The President's Day holiday gives them more spare time. They revisit the video game. The last time they played, the keys were won. The virtual zoo gate was opened. The letters G.G. appeared before the screen froze.

Sophia logs in. Her fairy avatar appears. The game is no longer frozen. The look is completely different. Sophia's Fairy princess is floating in a halo. Then the game background opens up as a split screen video. There are nine little blocks showing nine little videos playing all at the same time. The videos look like the zoo photos shown in the *Peninsula Review* article. This appears to be a live stream from different locations. Sophia can float her avatar from space to space. While floating over one of the video blocks, her bubble slips into that live stream. Her avatar now appears as part of the forest zoo. In this video block she sees a long-legged spotted dog run over to her avatar. The dog tries to sniff this strange visitor. Up! She floats, out of the dog's reach. Sophia stops playing and sends out a group text: *The game is a whole nother book! I think I need help with this.* Katie answers back, *when can we meet?* After a series of text messages, it is agreed that Sophia meeting at Katie's place is their only option. Katie, nervous about being the host, quickly cleans her room. Sophia puts her phone into her pocket. She finishes putting paper menus on the table in the restaurant patio. When she's done, she's allowed to go to Katie's. Sophia gets a ride over to her friend's place with a pizza.

The friends barely bite their food before sitting down to open their phones. The game shows Sophia's fairy is still floating around inside a clear circle. Katie logs on. Her hacker avatar appears inside the bubble.

Katie sends a group text to the rest of her friends. Ben responds: *Don't let the older kids in the neighborhood know this game is working.* The friends agree. Playing a game with a live zoo background is more interesting than getting the highest score. This now seems like THEIR private club. While playing the game, they can also see what is going on at the zoo. Their avatars pop in and out of squares and float against the zoo background. They try to gather items of value. Virtual rakes, scissors, bugs, fish and berries stick to their bubbles. The goal is to float off with the objects. When the items are dropped into virtual baskets, points are scored. Sophia's fairy avatar is the only one the animals seem to be able to see. All of the other avatars float around retrieving hidden virtual objects. They are unnoticed by the zoo's inhabitants. Sophia must take care not to pick up a virtual rake by a sleeping tiger. Sophia wonders why only her avatar projects her image into a real environment. Pulling virtual bugs out of a tree with the monkey close by doesn't seem like a good idea. She sends Katie a text: *Why am I the only one projecting?* Katie answers back: *It may be the camera your game is being played through. Let me ask.*

Back in Lucas' room, Kingston peeks out of his cardboard tube. He sees Lucas drop fresh bedding, water and seeds onto the floor of his glass house. Kingston is never quite sure of his little place. He misses the smells and variety of the woods. The University runs another article in the local paper. They announce the reintroduction of the pocket mouse family back into the restored zoo. The article explains that the zoo's exotic animals were found to be mostly self-sufficient and healthy while living on their own. Keeping the natural vegetation and water supply will provide the natural food sources. The thorny bushes remain. They are a refuge for little animals and birds from predators.

Lucas' family discusses the article over lunch. As Lucas looks down at his plate, his father reminds him that his friend is an endangered species. He takes a minute to think it over. Pocket mice can be solitary creatures. Being watched through glass may not be the way Kingston wants to live. Lucas knows his superpower is understanding nature. He agrees with his dad to put Kingston back. Lucas thinks he might see Kingston again while playing the Forest Zoo game.

Lucas' Father sends another email to the University. He asks if Kingston can be released into the Forest Zoo at the same time as the other pocket mice. The school responds with a time and date to meet.

Lucas sends Kingston's release time and date as a group text. The friends plan around this event. Sophia has mixed feelings. She hopes the zoo will provide safe places for their mouse to be. Yanu and Gwen agree.

The release day arrives. It is Wednesday afternoon. Sophia and Lucas send text reminders. On this day all eyes are on the zoo. They open their phones. The split screen shows the zoo's nine different views. The avatars floating in bubbles are less important than what is going on in the game background. One of the videos shows a tan four-wheel drive vehicle appearing. The door opens briefly and a man wearing a helmet steps out. He is carrying a box. After cautiously looking around, he sets the box near some rocks and bushes. The friends know exactly what is going on.

For Kingston, the air full of familiar smells is suddenly everywhere. Kingston runs from what others may consider as safe: fame. Royalty for him is less than thorny bush full of seeds and berries. He runs, jumps, and lands with excitement.

Chapter 17

National news reports a handful of the school's cameras have been compromised. The University responds to this news. The school reports that it is investigating the scale and scope of this issue. In a separate article, the University releases the hair sample results retrieved from the Forest Zoo fence. A picture of the sample described as "Thicker than human hair, thinner than horsetail" is shown. The microscopic study of the hair's root structure, and cuticle thickness match a polar bear thought to be extinct for 40,000 years. Yanu and her family find no relief in this discovery. The game warden verified the footprints made outside of her parent's window after the break in were not bear prints.

The hair sample article makes everyone curious. Gwen and Sophia ask Yanu if she has seen anything odd at her store. When Yanu gets home from Gwen's, she asks her parents to look at the photos. The ones taken the morning she found the keys. Her parents kept putting off the subject. After dinner, they agree to look at the pictures. A large unfocused, hairy form is seen by the steps. The shadowy figure is there, and then it isn't. The next few pictures were triggered by falling leaves. The pictures show snow accumulating, hiding any footprints. The next few photos show a small bump on the steps.

Because of the security breach, the friends quit the game for a while. It is hard to do as virtual visits to the Forest Zoo always show new things. Their game scores have never been higher.

The Zoo's hair sample test results are published. These results and the strange footprints cause concern. Playing by the creek is done with an adult present. The friends think this is too much caution, as the Forest Zoo has always been a bit odd.

It is a windless night. The farmer watches as his dogs stare into the direction of the Forest Zoo gate. A faint floral smell is hanging in the air. Seeing nothing, he brings the dogs inside and locks the door and goes to bed.

The next cool October morning, the farmer finds hoof and paw prints in the muddy field. A few pumpkins are smashed. The damage is not as severe as before.

Out of curiosity, the farmer follows the tracks. They lead into the woods. Broken twigs mark the path that was taken. The hoof and paw prints end at a strange place. The morning light shines through the crevice between two twisted trees. Squinting, he cannot believe the trail ends here.

Across the stream inside the zoo, Kingston is munching seeds. He is watching that place where sunlight seems to linger. This is where things show up.

Written by K. M. Keleher. The author has a B.S.N. from Carlow University, Pittsburgh, PA.

Art work by Tommy Ong. The artist has a Bachelor of Fine Arts, Morehead State University; Master of Fine Arts in 2D animation, Academy of Art University in San Francisco, CA.

Edited by Tom Kravitz. Bachelor of Arts in Writing, University of Pittsburgh.

The author, artist, and editor met in the Forest Zoo. They return now and then, when the need arises. Travel and nature inspire their work. They divide their time between California, Indonesia, and the Pacific Northwest. New discoveries fuel their storytelling.